JOHN WORSLEY

The illustrations by John Worsley in the *Award
Adventure Classics* series, have greatly added to the
impact and charm of these dramatic stories. Now
well-established as a portrait painter and marine ar-
tist, John Worsley was in the navy during the war.
Taken prisoner, he and a fellow officer constructed
an astonishingly life-like dummy to help in their
escape plan. After the war he was appointed adviser
to the makers of the famous war film, *Albert RN*,
which tells the true story of this remarkable feat.

ISBN 0 86163 068 8

Award Publications Limited 1982
Spring House, Spring Place
London NW5, England

© 1982 Victoria House Publishing

Printed in Belgium

Alexandre Dumas'
THE THREE MUSKETEERS

Retold by Jane Carruth

AWARD PUBLICATIONS — LONDON

On the road to Paris

IMAGINE, if you can, a young knight of eighteen, clothed not in a coat of mail but in a woollen doublet, the blue color of which had faded into some nameless shade between wine and azure.

Picture a young man with a face long and brown, high cheekbones, hooked nose and eyes bright and intelligent. There you have D'Artagnan!

If you had met him on the road you might perhaps have taken him for a farmer's son on a journey, had it not been for the long sword at his side and the cap, ornamented with a kind of feather, on his head. And if your eye had not been caught by his appearance, it would certainly have been attracted by the extraordinary looks of the horse he was riding. No bigger than a pony, it had a coat of bright yellow, and not a single hair in its tail!

D'Artagnan was a Gascon, proud and stubborn, with only one idea in his head — to join the Musketeers, the celebrated company of daring men pledged to serve the cause of France's king, Louis XIII. But today, the first Monday of the month of April 1625, there was an air of gloom on D'Artagnan's face as he jogged along.

Good horseman though he was, he was conscious of the ridiculous appearance he made mounted on such a ludicrous steed. Had not the pony been a parting gift from his old father, he would have refused to ride away on it. But not for the world would he have hurt the old man's feelings. Besides the pony, M. D'Artagnan the elder had presented him with money — fifteen crowns — and, most important of all, a letter of introduction to a certain M. de Tréville, captain of the musketeers and the third most important nobleman in France.

Having ridden long and hard for some time, D'Artagnan at length found himself at the gate of an inn where he decided to stop for refreshment. As he got down from his horse he noticed, through an open window on the ground floor, a man of fine figure, but with a grim face marred by an ugly scar on the temple, talking with two persons who appeared to be listening to him with great respect.

As was natural with D'Artagnan, he decided instantly that he himself was the object of their conversation and of their scornful looks. Pulling his cap down over his eyes and doing his best to copy some of the court airs he had picked up in Gascony among young travelling nobles, he advanced, with one hand on the hilt of his sword and the other resting on his hip.

"You, sir, who are hiding yourself behind that shutter, tell me what you are laughing at and we will laugh together!" he cried.

The stranger fixed him with a haughty stare and D'Artagnan saw that he was more than twice his own age, richly dressed in a doublet and hose of violet color. Then, moving away from the window, he came out of the inn with a slow step, and placed himself before the horse within two paces of the angry young man.

"This horse," he remarked, in a slow, insolent drawl, "must have been a buttercup in his youth. It is a color very well known in botany, but till the present time very rare among horses."

He had scarcely finished when D'Artagnan made such a furious lunge at him that if he had not sprung nimbly backwards it is probable that he would have jested for the last time.

The stranger then drew his own sword and placed himself on guard. But at that very moment his two companions, accom-panied by the innkeeper, fell upon D'Artagnan with sticks, shovels and tongs.

"A plague upon these Gascons! Put him on his yellow horse again and let him be gone!" cried the stranger, sheathing his sword.

"Not before I have killed you," shouted D'Artagnan, warding off the shower of blows that were now falling on him from every side.

The unequal fight went on for several more minutes until D'Artagnan, worn out, let fall his sword, which was struck from his hand by the blow of a stick and broken in two pieces. Another blow on his head at the same moment brought him to the ground, covered with blood and almost losing consciousness.

At this point, people came running to the scene from all sides. To avoid further disturbance, the innkeeper carried the

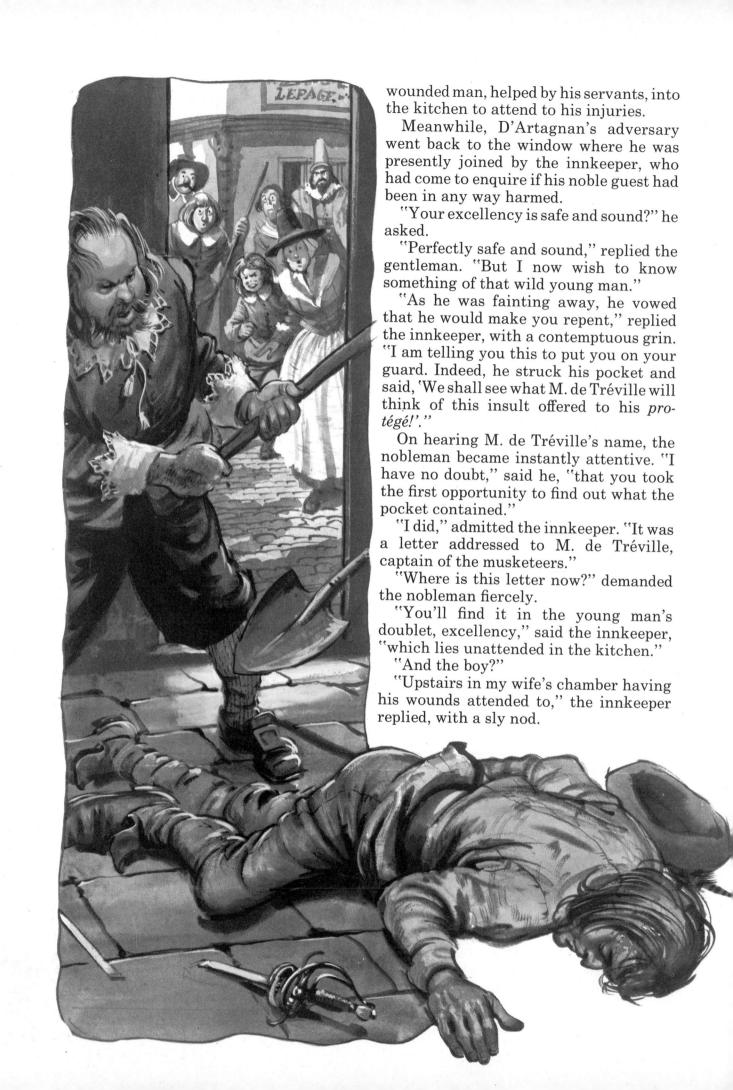

wounded man, helped by his servants, into the kitchen to attend to his injuries.

Meanwhile, D'Artagnan's adversary went back to the window where he was presently joined by the innkeeper, who had come to enquire if his noble guest had been in any way harmed.

"Your excellency is safe and sound?" he asked.

"Perfectly safe and sound," replied the gentleman. "But I now wish to know something of that wild young man."

"As he was fainting away, he vowed that he would make you repent," replied the innkeeper, with a contemptuous grin. "I am telling you this to put you on your guard. Indeed, he struck his pocket and said, 'We shall see what M. de Tréville will think of this insult offered to his *protégé!*'."

On hearing M. de Tréville's name, the nobleman became instantly attentive. "I have no doubt," said he, "that you took the first opportunity to find out what the pocket contained."

"I did," admitted the innkeeper. "It was a letter addressed to M. de Tréville, captain of the musketeers."

"Where is this letter now?" demanded the nobleman fiercely.

"You'll find it in the young man's doublet, excellency," said the innkeeper, "which lies unattended in the kitchen."

"And the boy?"

"Upstairs in my wife's chamber having his wounds attended to," the innkeeper replied, with a sly nod.

"My letter! My letter!" he cried in dismay. "Where is it?"

"Does the letter contain anything valuable?" asked the innkeeper.

"Indeed it does," said the young man, who counted on the letter to make his way at court. "It contained my whole fortune."

"That letter is not lost!" the innkeeper told him after a moment's hesitation. "It has been stolen from you by the gentleman who was here and with whom you fought. I am sure of it."

"Then he is a thief," shouted D'Artagnan angrily. "He has not seen the last of me."

He then drew two crowns majestically from his purse, gave them to the innkeeper, who accompanied him to the gate, remounted his yellow horse and galloped off in the direction of Paris. Arriving there without any further mishap, he sold his horse for three crowns, and entered France's capital city on foot. He soon found a garret both suitable to his means and near the hotel where M. de Tréville lived.

His next task was to have a new blade put on his sword, and when this was done he retired to bed and slept the sleep of the brave.

As he left the room his guest, grim-faced, rose to his feet. There was little doubt in the innkeeper's mind that he would soon find his way to the kitchen.

The following morning at five o'clock, D'Artagnan rose and went down to the kitchen without help and, refusing any assistance, replaced the bandages on his wounds. That same evening he was able to walk about, and the next morning had almost recovered.

But when the time came to settle his bill, D'Artagnan found nothing in his pocket but his worn little velvet purse with the crowns. The letter addressed to M. de Tréville had disappeared.

The Captain of the Musketeers

M. DE TRÉVILLE, on whose patronage D'Artagnan had pinned all his hopes, was not only captain of the king's musketeers, but one of the most powerful men at court apart from Cardinal de Richelieu, his most bitter rival for the king's favor.

The cardinal, too, had his own guards, and the rivalry between the two companies led to duels and broils which were often fought to the death.

Frequently half-drunk, the king's musketeers — or rather, M. de Tréville's — could be seen lounging in the taverns, in the parks and at public sports, shouting, twisting their moustaches, clanking their swords, and taking great pleasure in annoying the guards of the cardinal whenever they could. But ruffians though they were, they adored their captain and were always ready to sacrifice themselves to wipe out the least insult to him.

The court of M. de Tréville's hotel was like a camp, with some fifty to sixty musketeers parading up and down, armed to the teeth, shouting and quarrelling.

The day on which D'Artagnan presented himself at the hotel remained long in his memory. At the center of the noisiest group of men was a musketeer of great height, with a haughty expression and dressed in a costume so peculiar as to attract general attention. He did not wear the uniform cloak, but a blue doublet, a little faded and worn, and over this a magnificent baldric worked in gold. A long cloak of crimson velvet fell in graceful folds from his shoulders, revealing in front the splendid baldric, from which hung a gigantic rapier.

While D'Artagnan hovered on the fringe of the group, he learnt that the name of this magnificent musketeer was Porthos. But he was more immediately attracted to the young man at his side, who surely could be only a few years older than himself. The two were in perfect contrast, for he was portly in build, with a fair, delicate face, and a voice and manner as soft and gentle as a woman's.

Hearing Porthos address him as Aramis, D'Artagnan took note of the name.

Having asked a servant to find out when M. de Tréville would see him, D'Artagnan waited expectantly to be summoned into the captain's office, and was rather embarrassed when presently the servant returned, and said loudly, "M. de Tréville awaits M. D'Artagnan."

In the sudden hush which followed the servant's announcement, D'Artagnan crossed the antechamber, and entered the apartment of the captain of the musketeers.

After politely saluting the young man, M. de Tréville went to the door and called loudly, "Athos! Porthos! Aramis!"

The two musketeers whom D'Artagnan already knew left the group and entered the office. After their captain had paced up and down in silence once or twice, he suddenly turned upon them angrily.

"Do you know what the king said to me?" he cried. "Do you, gentlemen?"

"No," replied the two musketeers, who were standing as if on parade.

"He told me that from now on he would recruit his musketeers from among the guards of the cardinal."

The two musketeers colored up to the eyes, and D'Artagnan would have liked the ground to swallow him up.

"Yes, yes," continued M. de Tréville, growing angrier every minute. "And no wonder, for it seems my brave musketeers allowed themselves to be arrested by the cardinal's guards."

"The truth is, captain," said Porthos, quite beside himself, "we were not captured by fair means. Before we had time to draw our swords two of our party were dead and Athos grievously wounded. We did not surrender; we were dragged away

by force, and were shortly able to make our escape."

"Athos was left for dead, sir," Aramis put in, "and indeed his wound is very serious."

At this instant the door opened and a young man with a noble, handsome face, but frightfully pale, appeared before them.

"Athos!" cried the two musketeers.

"You sent for me, sir," said Athos to the captain. "I am here, sir. What do you want with me?"

Moved by the young man's courage, M. de Tréville seized his hand. "I was about to say to these gentlemen," he cried, "that I forbid my brave musketeers to risk their lives needlessly, for brave men are dear to the king."

Athos was by this time as pale as a corpse; he began to sway on his feet, then fell to the ground where he lay as though dead.

M. de Tréville immediately opened the door for Porthos and Aramis to carry off their comrade in their arms. When they had gone, the captain turned to D'Artagnan. "I loved your father very much," said he. "What can I do for his son?"

Without more ado, D'Artagnan launched into his story of the letter of recommendation written by his father, and described in minutest detail the villain who had stolen it.

The captain listened with the closest attention. "I know this man!" he cried, at length. "And you must beware of him. Do not cast yourself against such a rock; he will break you like glass."

Then, leaving his *protégé* by the window, he sat down at the table to write a letter of recommendation to the king. Having written the letter and sealed it, he rose and went over to the window to give it to him. But at the very moment that D'Artagnan stretched out his hand to receive it, he amazed the captain by turning crimson with fury, and with a sudden spring rushed from the room shouting, "Ah, he shall not escape me this time. Thief! Traitor! Vengeance is mine!"

Into battle

IN HIS FURY, D'Artagnan bounded out of the room and down the stairs, running head-first into a musketeer who was coming out of one of the captain's private rooms.

"You are in a hurry," said the musketeer, as pale as a sheet, and he grabbed hold of D'Artagnan by his scarf.

"Let me go!" protested D'Artagnan furiously.

"It is easy to see that you come from a distance," returned Athos — for that was who it was. "You have forgotten your manners!" But he released the scarf.

"If I were not in such haste . . ." seethed D'Artagnan, fingering his sword.

"Mr Man-in-a-hurry, you can find me any time," said Athos softly.

"And where, I pray you?"

"Near the convent of the Carmes-Deschaux."

"At what hour?"

"About noon."

"Good," cried D'Artagnan, "I will be there!"

And he set off again, running as if the devil possessed him. At the street gate Porthos was talking with the soldier on guard. D'Artagnan sprang forward like a dart between them and as he did so, the wind blew out Porthos's long cloak, and he rushed straight into the middle of it.

"Good Lord!" Porthos cried, trying to rid himself of D'Artagnan, but refusing to let go the flap. "The fellow's mad . . ."

"Not mad!" D'Artagnan laughed, reappearing under the shoulder of the giant. "Merely in a hurry. But you surprise me, sir, for though you look so fine in front, your back is most shabbily clad!"

Foaming with rage that the poorness of his dress, which his cloak normally con-cealed, should have been discovered, Porthos rushed after the young Gascon. "You will pay for your impertinence!" he shouted.

"Not now," cried D'Artagnan, over his shoulder. "Later!"

"At one o'clock, then, behind the Lux-embourg," answered Porthos furiously.

"Very well," replied D'Artagnan, as he rounded the corner of the street.

His enemy had by this time disappeared and, with a disappointed shrug, D'Artagnan decided to return to his rooms. On the way, he saw Aramis chat-ting gaily with three gentlemen of the king's guards. His salutation was coldly received and he was just preparing to retreat when he noticed that Aramis had just let his handerchief fall and by mis-

take, no doubt, had placed his foot upon it.

With the most gracious air he could muster, D'Artagnan bent down and drew the handkerchief, delicately perfumed and edged with fine lace, from under the foot of the musketeer, who seemed determined to continue standing on it.

"Sir," said Aramis, refusing to accept the handkerchief, which D'Artagnan could now clearly see must belong to a lady, "you are a fool. People do not tread upon pocket-handkerchiefs without good reason."

"You do me wrong," said D'Artagnan, whose quarrelsome nature began immediately to get the upper hand. "There is no call to be insulting."

"You have compromised a lady," replied Aramis. "You have now made it known that I carry her handkerchief. I see that I must teach you how to behave towards a musketeer. At two o'clock I will expect you at the hotel of M. de Tréville. There I will point out to you the best place and time."

The two young men bowed and separated, Aramis turning in the direction of Luxembourg, while D'Artagnan, seeing that it was almost noon, took the road to Carmes-Deschaux, saying to himself, "Decidedly I can't draw back, but at least if I am killed I shall be killed by a musketeer!"

When D'Artagnan arrived at the bare spot of ground close to the monastery, Athos had been waiting about five minutes. He was seated on a stone but, at the sight of D'Artagnan, he rose and advanced to meet him. On his part, the young Gascon saluted him with hat in hand, his feather touching the ground.

"Sir," said Athos, "my two friends, who will act as seconds, have not yet arrived . . ."

But even as he spoke the giant figure of Porthos appeared from one direction and that of Aramis from another.

"What!" cried D'Artagnan, in great astonishment, "Are these your seconds?"

Before Athos could reply, Porthos came up to them and pointing at D'Artagnan said, "But I am fighting this gentleman myself . . ."

"But not before one o'clock," said D'Artagnan.

"I too have engaged him in a duel," said Aramis, as he joined the group.

"But not till two o'clock," said D'Artagnan.

And with a gallant air, he drew his sword, and requested Athos, still deathly pale from his former wounds, to stand on guard.

Scarcely had the two rapiers clashed when a company of the cardinal's guards, commanded by M. de Jussac, rode into view.

"The cardinal's guards!" cried Porthos. "Sheathe swords, gentlemen!"

But it was too late.

"Halloo!" cried Jussac, advancing towards them. "Duelling is forbidden, as you well know. I arrest you in the name of the king."

"Pass on your way," said Aramis, with deceptive politeness.

"We will charge you if you disobey," replied Jussac angrily.

"We are but three against five," Porthos muttered, "but we fight."

"Gentlemen," said D'Artagnan, "let me correct you. You are four against five!"

Without more ado, the three musketeers charged, with D'Artagnan at their side. They fought like mad tigers, and as the battle began going their way, Jussac aimed a terrible thrust at D'Artagnan, who parried it and, while Jussac was recovering himself, glided like a serpent beneath his blade, and passed his sword through Jussac's body.

With Jussac out of the battle and one guardsman killed by Aramis, there was no doubt how it would eventually end. Finally, the sergeant of the guards commanded his remaining men to stop fighting. As they were all wounded and in desperate straits, this was no cowardly decision.

Shouting with joy at the way the battle had gone, the three musketeers warmly embraced D'Artagnan, who had fought like ten men, and then made their way to the hotel of M. de Tréville to give an account of their victory.

One for all, all for one!

AFTER SUCH A victory, it was inevitable that D'Artagnan should be hailed as a true compatriot and friend by the three musketeers.

"You must get yourself a lackey," Porthos told him, "a man who will see to your needs and serve you faithfully."

To this D'Artagnan agreed though he, like his friends, was desperately short of money. That very day, Porthos found him Planchet, a fellow he met upon a bridge, spitting in the water to make rings!

Athos, too, had a valet. Named Grimaud, he said little and never laughed, yet he understood his master perfectly.

But by far the most unusual of the servants was Mousqueton, who had entered Porthos' service on the understanding that he should always be clothed and housed in a very handsome manner. He asked no payment for his services — only that he should be given two hours' freedom every day to go about his own business.

The oldest of the lackeys was Bazin, who served Aramis. It had always been accepted by the musketeers that Aramis would one day become a priest and Bazin, out of respect for his master's future career in the church, always dressed in sober black.

The four young men had come to lead very similar lives. D'Artagnan, who had no fixed habits of his own, did everything his three friends did, even mounting guard with them, and they with him, when he was on duty.

One fine morning, D'Artagnan received word that he had become a cadet in the Chevalier des Essarts and that within two years he would become a musketeer. But to that impatient young man two years seemed a very long time indeed to have to wait, and he resolved he would do what he could to prove himself worthy of being a musketeer long before that.

Meantime, the four friends were becoming desperately short of money. Aramis had sold some of his precious books on religion to provide money for their food.

Now it was D'Artagnan's turn to find some funds. He was sitting in his garret racking his brain to think of some means to obtain money when someone tapped gently at his door.

The stout little man who entered looked like an elderly tradesman. "I have heard," he said, bowing to D'Artagnan, "that you are a very brave young man, and I have made up my mind to let you into a secret."

"Speak on, man," said D'Artagnan, who was instantly intrigued. "Speak on!"

"I have a young and very beautiful wife," his visitor continued, "who is seamstress to the queen. Well, sir, to be

brief — she was carried off yesterday morning as she came out of her work-room."

"By whom?" D'Artagnan demanded. "Have you seen him?"

The stranger nodded. "My wife pointed him out to me one day. He is one of the cardinal's henchmen — a wicked, desperate man, I have reason to believe, though I do not know his name."

"Would you recognize him again?" D'Artagnan asked eagerly.

"Most certainly; he has a haughty face, piercing eyes and an ugly scar on his temple . . ."

"A scar on his temple!" cried D'Artagnan. "Haughty, you say! Why, that is *my* man! Tell me your own name, good sir. I will help you."

"Bonacieux," replied his visitor, "your landlord, noble sir, and one who, if I may say so, has not overburdened you with requests for payment of rent."

D'Artagnan nodded. "Now, tell me," he said, "why should he take your wife?"

"She is close to the queen," answered Bonacieux, "and very loyal and devoted to her. A M. de la Porte, her godfather, has warned me that she may be in danger from the cardinal's men. Believe me, sir, the cardinal will do anything to bring about disgrace to the queen."

"I understand," said D'Artagnan. "I will do whatever has to be done to save your lady-wife — and at the same time avenge myself."

"And for your services," said M. Bonacieux, making for the door, "you shall live rent-free in my house for as long as you wish."

When M. Bonacieux had gone, Athos, Porthos and Aramis arrived at D'Artagnan's chamber, and the young man set out immediately to acquaint them with his forthcoming adventure.

"All for one, one for all!" said Porthos, after the story had been told. "We are all in this together."

"That is well!" cried D'Artagnan, greatly delighted. "Now let us retire — each to his own house — to think on the matter. Remember, from this moment we are at war with the cardinal!"

Before they could leave the house, however, some of the cardinal's soldiers appeared. D'Artagnan made no effort to save his landlord as they dragged him away, protesting. "They must not suspect on whose side I am," he told his three friends. "With Bonacieux in prison, I shall have more freedom to make my own investigation."

The plot thickens

THE NEXT DAY, D'Artagnan quickly learnt from his faithful servant, Planchet, that the cardinal's men were actually keeping watch from inside the house.

"It is a trap, sir," said Planchet, "for whoever enters is immediately arrested and questioned."

That very same night, D'Artagnan, having made a peephole in the floor immediately above the room used by the cardinal's men, heard loud cries of distress, and immediately stretched out on the floor to find out who had walked into the trap.

Despite his prudence, he could scarcely hold himself back from rushing downstairs to rescue the pretty young woman being questioned.

"I tell you I *am* Madame Bonacieux!" he heard her cry. "I belong to the queen."

"Quick, Planchet!" he whispered. "Run

and get Athos, Porthos, and Aramis. Tell them to arm themselves. I'm going down by the window, in order to save the lady. They are beginning to drag her away." And crossing to the window, he climbed out, let himself fall from the first storey, and was lucky enough to land without injury.

Going straight to the door of the room which held the young woman, he rushed in, sword in hand. His sudden entrance took the men by surprise, and though they tried to defend themselves with chairs, stools and crockery, they were too frightened to put up much of a fight, and with cries of terror took to their heels.

On being left alone with Madame Bonacieux, D'Artagnan turned towards her. He saw she was a charming woman, a few years older than himself, with dark hair, blue eyes and a pink complexion.

She held out her hands to him with so sweet a smile that D'Artagnan immediately lost his heart to her. "You have saved me, sir," she said softly. "I thank you."

"Madame," replied D'Artagnan, kissing her hand, "these men were more dangerous than robbers. They are the cardinal's agents, and already they have put your husband in the Bastille."

"Poor dear man!" cried Madame Bonacieux. "He is innocence itself!" But she did not seem as distressed as D'Artagnan expected her to be.

"Dear lady," D'Artagnan continued, "we must fly from this house while we can. I will take you to my friend's house. Athos will care for you while I carry out your commands."

"You must go to M. de la Porte," she told him. "He is the queen's valet and lives only to serve her. Send him to me."

After having safely delivered Madame Bonacieux to his friend's house, D'Artagnan found M. de la Porte and told him where to find her. Then he went home.

As he was arriving at the end of the Rue Guenegaud he saw, coming out of a side street, two persons whose appearance caught his attention. One was a man, in the uniform of a musketeer, and the other,

in a hooded cloak, a woman: Madame Bonacieux.

Already in love with her, D'Artagnan felt that she had betrayed him. As they passed beneath a lamp, he sprang forward.

"What do you want?" demanded the lady's escort advancing a step and pushing D'Artagnan aside with his hand.

D'Artagnan drew his sword.

"In the name of heaven, milord," cried Madame Bonacieux, throwing herself between the two men.

"Milord!" cried D'Artagnan, suddenly gripped by an idea. "Pardon me, sir . . ."

"Milord, the Duke of Buckingham," said Madame Bonacieux, "Prime Minister to the king of England, and our queen's devoted admirer. If Cardinal de

"I have given you no encouragement," whispered the queen. "You risk death in coming here, to risk so much . . ."

"Give me some favor — something you have worn, so that I may have something of yours to take back to England," pleaded the Duke, rising to his feet.

"Will you go then, if I give you what you ask for?" asked the queen, tenderly.

"Yes!"

Anne of Austria went into her apartment and came out again almost immediately, holding a casket in her hand.

"You will find a necklace in this casket which I have worn many times," she said. "Take it and go."

Buckingham accepted the casket, raised the queen's beautiful hands to his lips, then rushed out of the apartment.

Madame Bonacieux was waiting for him, and led him safely out of the Louvre.

Richelieu should discover that he is here . . ." she broke off, then added bitterly, "You may have ruined us all."

"A hundred pardons," said D'Artagnan humbly. "I serve the queen, and, milord, that means I serve you."

"Then follow us at a distance of twenty paces to the Louvre," said Buckingham, smiling at him. "We are in your hands."

D'Artagnan, sword unsheathed, did as he was requested, waiting until he saw the couple go into the palace before leaving.

Meanwhile, Madame Bonacieux led the disguised duke across the courtyard to a servants' entrance. And, after guiding him up several flights of stairs and along several corridors, left him. The Duke walked on alone until presently a door concealed in the tapestry opened, and a woman appeared. It was the queen.

Anne of Austria advanced two steps and Buckingham threw himself at her feet, and kissed the hem of her robe.

"Madame," he whispered, his handsome face radiant, "you know that you have my undying love . . ."

The fatal necklace

IF WE ARE to understand what happened next and how D'Artagnan found himself engaged in the major adventure of his life, we must first consider the second most important man in France, the Cardinal de Richelieu.

Although the cardinal was a friend of the king's, he was by no means friendly towards the queen, whose influence over Louis he sought to destroy by all possible means.

It was he who had arranged the arrest of Madame Bonacieux's husband, believing quite rightly that Madame Bonacieux was in the confidence of the queen of France.

Once he had Bonacieux in his power, the cardinal quickly discovered that the

fat little landlord had no knowledge of his pretty young wife's affairs. And he persuaded him that he would be doing his country a great service if he would faithfully report all that went on under his roof. To this M. Bonacieux agreed, never suspecting that the wily cardinal was merely using him.

"In that case," said the cardinal at the end of the interview, "you are free to go, and here are a hundred pistoles to compensate you for the time you have spent in the Bastille."

But as the grateful landlord left the cardinal, he saw a face he would not forget easily — a face disfigured with a scar on the temple, and now for the first time he had a name to put to it — Rochefort — for the cardinal greeted the newcomer by this name as Bonacieux left the room.

Rochefort was one of the cardinal's most trusted secret agents, a ruthless man prepared to go to any lengths to please his master. No sooner did he find himself alone with the Cardinal than he began to report on Madame Bonacieux's activities.

"My agent inside the Louvre," said he, "has told me much concerning this Madame Bonacieux and of the part she played in bringing the Duke of Buckingham to the queen."

The cardinal's keen eyes glinted at the

mention of the queen. "Go on, Count," he urged. "I suspected the duke was in Paris."

"The queen saw him and gave him a casket," Rochefort continued, "a casket which contained the very necklace of twelve diamond studs which the king presented to her on her birthday."

"And which, no doubt," said the cardinal, "is now in Buckingham's palace in England."

"We have the Comtesse de Winter already installed in his palace," Rochefort pointed out. "She is, as you know, your eminence, one of our most trusted agents . . ."

"And as cunning and ambitious as any man," interrupted the cardinal.

Milady
Be at the first Ball at which the Duke of Buckingham shall be

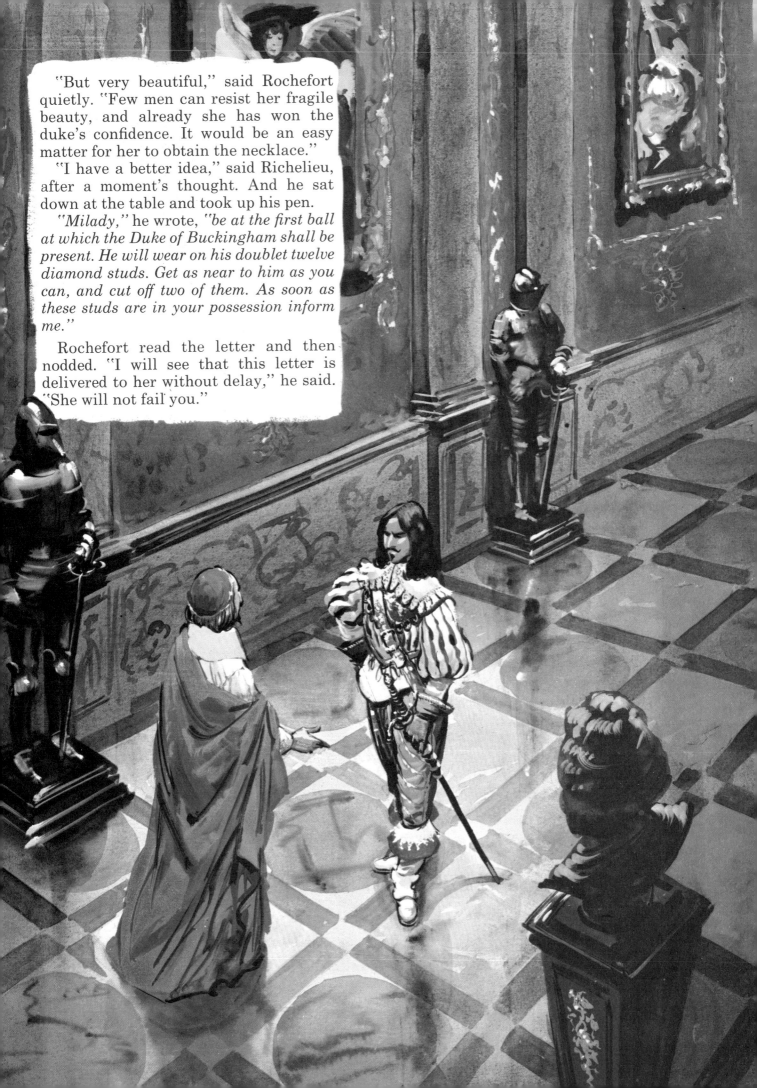

"But very beautiful," said Rochefort quietly. "Few men can resist her fragile beauty, and already she has won the duke's confidence. It would be an easy matter for her to obtain the necklace."

"I have a better idea," said Richelieu, after a moment's thought. And he sat down at the table and took up his pen.

"*Milady*," he wrote, "*be at the first ball at which the Duke of Buckingham shall be present. He will wear on his doublet twelve diamond studs. Get as near to him as you can, and cut off two of them. As soon as these studs are in your possession inform me.*"

Rochefort read the letter and then nodded. "I will see that this letter is delivered to her without delay," he said. "She will not fail you."

That same day the cardinal sought an interview with the king. "Your Majesty," said he, "I have good reason to believe that our common enemy, the Duke of Buckingham, has been in Paris these last few days . . ."

Louis XIII, turning pale, burst out, "Why did you not have him arrested? What brought him here? I tell you it was to see the queen. She loves Buckingham."

"We have no proof that they met," said the cardinal soothingly, "but there is, your Majesty, a simple way to make sure."

"What? Tell me!" burst out the jealous king.

"Give a ball," replied the cardinal. "You know how much the queen loves dancing." Then he added, with a meaningful smile, "And, sire, do not forget to tell her Majesty that you would like to see her

wearing the diamond studs you gave her for her birthday."

No sooner had the cardinal departed than Louis sought out the queen. "Madame," he began, "I intend holding a ball shortly. It is my wish — nay, my command — that you attend in state dress, wearing the diamond studs which I gave you."

Anne of Austria looked at the king with sudden terror in her eyes, unable to utter a single syllable. And Louis, enjoying her distress, but without guessing the true reason for it, bowed and left her.

Left alone, the queen began sobbing loudly, and it was in this pitiful state that Madame Bonacieux found her.

"Madame," cried she, falling on her knees, "how can I serve you? You know I am ready to die for your Majesty."

"I must get the diamond studs back from the duke," whispered the queen. "But how? How?"

"Someone must be sent to England — to the Duke of Buckingham," replied the young woman. "Trust me, Madame. I will find a messenger."

"I must write to him," murmured the queen. "He must know the reason." And

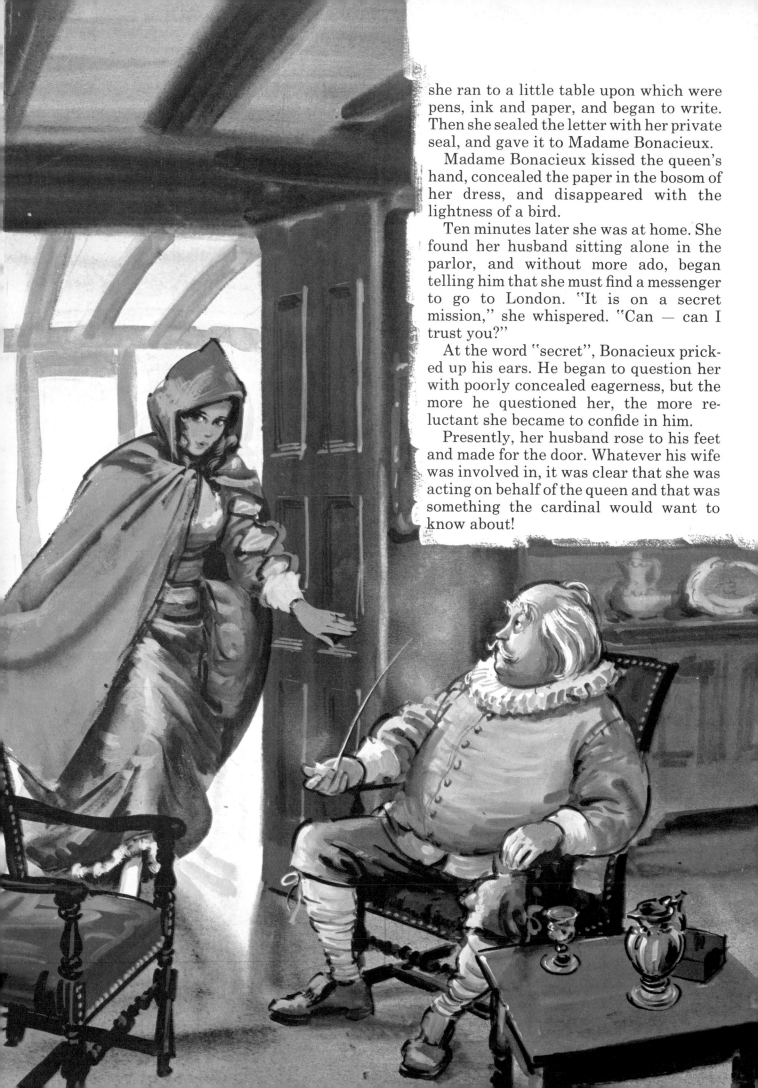

she ran to a little table upon which were pens, ink and paper, and began to write. Then she sealed the letter with her private seal, and gave it to Madame Bonacieux.

Madame Bonacieux kissed the queen's hand, concealed the paper in the bosom of her dress, and disappeared with the lightness of a bird.

Ten minutes later she was at home. She found her husband sitting alone in the parlor, and without more ado, began telling him that she must find a messenger to go to London. "It is on a secret mission," she whispered. "Can — can I trust you?"

At the word "secret", Bonacieux pricked up his ears. He began to question her with poorly concealed eagerness, but the more he questioned her, the more reluctant she became to confide in him.

Presently, her husband rose to his feet and made for the door. Whatever his wife was involved in, it was clear that she was acting on behalf of the queen and that was something the cardinal would want to know about!

If her husband could not be trusted, where was Madame Bonacieux to find a messenger? As she sat alone by the window, the answer came in the shape of the handsome young cavalier who had rescued her from the cardinal's men — no less a person than D'Artagnan, who now entered the room.

"Madame," D'Artagnan began, with a deep bow, "I overheard most of that conversation. Look no further for a messenger. I am your man."

Madame Bonacieux's heart beat with joy, and a secret hope shone in her eyes. Finally, she said, "What pledge can you give me if I confide this message to you?"

"My love for you and my devotion to the queen," replied the young man.

As if satisfied by his answer, the young woman went to the cupboard, took from it a bag filled with pistoles and handed it to D'Artagnan. Then she gave him the queen's letter.

"There is money enough in the bag to buy your passage to England," she said. "Once there, make for the Duke of Buckingham's palace with all haste and give him this letter. Remember that the queen's well-being, perhaps even her life, is at stake."

"For her and for you!" cried D'Artagnan, his eyes alight with excitement. "Trust me!"

And he ran from the apartment.

The journey

IF YOU HAD happened to be up and about early the following morning, you would have seen D'Artagnan with his three friends ride out of the city, attended by their lackeys, and heavily armed.

All went well as far as Chantilly, where they stopped at an inn for breakfast and where, alas, the giant Porthos entered into an argument with a stranger just as they were leaving.

"I must stay behind and fight it out," he told the others. "Ride on. I will catch you up."

So the travellers continued on their way. After about two hours' ride, they fell in with a company of about eight men who appeared to be employed in digging holes and making muddy ruts in the narrow road.

Athos reprimanded them sharply, and the men immediately drew back to the ditch, from which each took a concealed musket and began firing.

"It is an ambush!" shouted D'Artagnan. "Don't waste a shot. Forward!"

Aramis was wounded in the shoulder, and Mousqueton was knocked off his horse. But nevertheless D'Artagnan dared not stop with so much at stake. Soon it became clear, however, that he would not be able to count on Aramis' support for long, so weak had he become through loss of blood. When they reached Crèvecoeur, they left Aramis at the first inn they came upon, and Bazin stayed behind to take care of him.

Then, anxious to make up time lost, D'Artagnan, Athos and the two lackeys set off again. By midnight, they were in Amiens, at the inn of the Golden Lily.

The innkeeper, with his candlestick in one hand and his cotton nightcap in the other, admitted the travellers.

"Grimaud can take care of the horses," said Planchet. "If you are willing, gentlemen, I will sleep across your doorway, and you will then be certain that nobody can surprise you."

But no more than two hours later, the adventurers were roused by cries for help and, on rushing down to the stables, found Grimaud lying senseless on the ground, with his head split open by a blow from one of the stable-boys.

"I believe this is all part of a wicked plot to delay us on our journey," cried D'Artagnan, greatly distressed. "Pay the

reckoning, Athos, and let us be gone."

But when Athos paid the innkeeper, he turned the pistoles over in his hand, then began shouting that the money was bad.

"Arrest these men as counterfeiters!" he cried, as four well-armed men entered by the side doors and rushed upon Athos.

"I am taken!" Athos shouted loudly. "Go on, D'Artagnan! Go! Go!"

D'Artagnan and Planchet did not require a second bidding. They unfastened the two horses that were waiting at the door, leapt upon them, buried their spurs in the horses' sides, and set off at full gallop.

On reaching the port, they found a vessel ready to sail for England, and five minutes later they were on board.

As soon as they were safely arrived in London, D'Artagnan, though unable to speak much English, quickly discovered the whereabouts of the duke's palace, and presently found himself in the presence of England's most important minister.

No sooner had Buckingham read the queen's letter than he realized what was at stake, and bidding the young cavalier follow him, he walked rapidly through several apartments, furnished with an elegance which astonished D'Artagnan, until he arrived at length in a bedchamber which was a miracle of wealth and splendor. In a tapestried alcove of this chamber was a door which the duke opened with a small gold key suspended from his neck by a chain of the same metal.

"Here," he said, drawing from the casket a large bow of blue ribbon all sparkling with diamonds, "here are the precious studs. I have sworn an oath that they should be buried with me."

Then he began to kiss, one after the other, those studs with which he was about to part. All at once he uttered a terrible cry.

"What is the matter, milord?" exclaimed D'Artagnan anxiously.

"All is lost! All is lost!" cried Buckingham, as white as a sheet. "Two of the studs are missing — there are but ten of them

left! It is the cardinal's doing! See how the ribbons which held them have been cut."

"When did you last wear them, milord?" asked D'Artagnan. "Can you remember?"

"The only time I wore them was at a ball given by the king a week ago. The Comtesse de Winter, I recall, admired them excessively. Yes, yes, it is she who must have taken them, for she is an agent of the cardinal's."

"We have but five days to recover them," said D'Artagnan. "What can we do?"

"Five days!" cried Buckingham, regaining some of his composure. "That's more time than we need!" And going to the door, he summoned his personal valet, ordering him to bring his jeweller and his secretary to him at once.

The secretary arrived within minutes, and Buckingham, who had been busily writing, said, "Ah, Master Jackson, go instantly to the Lord Chancellor with this order, to be executed without delay."

As he spoke, the duke signed the paper with a flourish and handed it to his secretary, who then bowed and went out.

"We are safe on that side!" exclaimed Buckingham, turning to D'Artagnan. "If the studs are not yet gone to Paris, they will not arrive till after you, for I have just placed an embargo on all vessels at present in his Majesty's ports. Not one will dare to raise anchor without my permission."

As he finished speaking, the goldsmith entered the room, and the duke addressed him directly.

"Master O'Reilly," said he, "look at these diamond studs, and tell me how many days you would require to make two studs exactly like them."

"A week, your grace."

"I will give you a hundred times their weight in gold if I can have them by the day after tomorrow."

"Your grace, you shall have them," promised the jeweller, who was the finest goldsmith in the country.

D'Artagnan spent the next two days in a state of deep anxiety. When he was finally summoned into the duke's presence, his

face showed the strain under which he had been living.

"Here," said Buckingham, without preamble, "are the diamond studs, and so perfectly fashioned that they are exact imitations. No one could tell the new ones from the old."

"You are right, milord," D'Artagnan exclaimed, accepting the studs. "They are perfect imitations."

"Now go!" said the duke. "At the port, ask for the brig *Le Sund,* and give this letter to the captain. He will convey you to a little port where certainly no one is on the watch for you."

D'Artagnan bowed and left the palace. Without wasting a moment, he collected Planchet, and together they set out for the port where they embarked on the brig.

The next day, he was safely in Paris.

Mission completed

THE BALL, which was to be held in the City Hall, was the talk of Paris the following day.

By midnight the city was alive with eager, jostling crowds who had come to watch the royal procession pass through the streets. No sooner did the king arrive, however, than the cardinal drew him aside and placed in his hand a casket containing two diamond studs.

"What does this mean?" Louis demanded.

"Nothing," replied the cardinal, "but if the queen is wearing the studs, count them carefully, sire, and if you find only ten, ask her where the other two can be."

Just then came a shout of admiration from the assembly as Anne of Austria appeared wearing the costume of a huntress, which suited her admirably. The king trembled with joy, and the cardinal with vexation, as they saw on her left shoulder the sparkle of diamond studs, mounted on a bow in the same shade of blue as the plumes of her hat and petticoat.

Before the king had an opportunity to count the studs, the violins struck up, and he was obliged to lead the President's wife on to the floor. At the end of the dance he approached Anne with barely concealed haste, holding out the two studs he had been given by the cardinal.

The young queen pretended great surprise. "Why, sire," she exclaimed, "you wish me to have two more studs! Now I shall have fourteen."

"So it would seem," replied the king, hurriedly counting the diamonds on their ribbons. He called the cardinal to him.

The cardinal, biting his lip, began at once to explain that he did indeed intend her Majesty to have two more studs, but had not dared to presume to present them to her himself!

Some hours later, the young hero of the hour, D'Artagnan, was about to retire when he was approached by Madame Bonacieux, wearing a black velvet mask. She signalled him to follow her. Moved by both love and curiosity, D'Artagnan did so, and presently found himself in a closet, which was quite dark. She then opened a second door concealed by a tapestry, which, as it was drawn aside, let in a sudden flood of brilliant light. Then she disappeared.

At length, a hand and slender white arm appeared from behind the tapestry, and D'Artagnan understood that he was to receive his reward. He cast himself on his knees, took the hand, and kissed it respectfully. The hand was then withdrawn, leaving in his own a ring.

As soon as he could, D'Artagnan made certain that his three loyal friends were safe and well, and his relief was considerable when he found that they had each recovered from their separate ordeals. They rejoiced with him at the success of his mission, and remarked on the magnificent diamond ring which he now wore, but about which he would give no explanation.

The pretty little Madame Bonacieux filled most of D'Artagnan's waking thoughts. Imagine his anguish, therefore, when he discovered that for a second time she had been spirited away.

In his frantic efforts to discover her kidnappers, D'Artagnan came into contact with an enemy more dangerous and vengeful than the agent Rochefort himself — the beautiful Comtesse de Winter. She had brought the two diamond studs to Paris and given them to the cardinal, only to find all her efforts to please Richelieu and win for herself a substantial reward had come to nothing — on account of the young cavalier and Madame Bonacieux. And she determined to destroy them both.

D'Artagnan might well have been fooled by the flattering attention she paid him, whenever they met, had he not been warned of her true nature. And he was soon to learn that she had played an important part in his beloved's disappearance.

"I must be constantly on my guard against her," he told Athos, "for she is still Rochefort's trusted accomplice."

"Make no mistake, my friend," Athos told him quietly. "She will avenge herself on you, in her own good time."

The eavesdroppers

EVENTS NOW took an unexpected turn in the lives of the four friends. They awoke one day to find themselves under marching orders. The enemy was no foreign invader but the Calvinist rebels at Rochelle, whose port was the last in the kingdom of France open to the English.

The king was in as much haste to attack and take Rochelle as the cardinal, for he shared his hatred for Buckingham, who openly supported the Calvinists.

D'Artagnan and the three musketeers, armed to the hilt and ready for anything, were by no means unhappy at finding themselves involved in a battle which, in their opinion, could not last for long. Meanwhile, once the soldiers had made camp, there was plenty of time for pursuing their own private pleasures.

One day, while D'Artagnan was in the trenches, Athos, Porthos and Aramis were called upon to escort the cardinal to a certain tavern. On arrival, he immediately disappeared to an upper room, leaving the three friends in the taproom.

As they waited for him Athos pointed suddenly to a stovepipe, broken in half. The top end of it went through to the upper chamber. Bending down, he pressed his ear to the pipe and motioned his friends to be silent. It was now perfectly possible to overhear the conversation taking place in the room above them.

"Listen, milady," the cardinal was saying, "You must go at once to London and seek out Buckingham. No doubt he views you with grave suspicion since the affair of the diamond studs, but no matter. He will listen to you."

"What must I tell him?" asked the Comtesse de Winter.

"Tell him if he sends an English fleet to Rochelle, I will ruin the queen."

There was a moment's silence, then all three heard milady's voice again. "I have but one favor to ask," she said. "Rid me

of one who has already done our cause great harm, and I will be well content."

"You mean . . .?"

"I mean D'Artagnan," replied milady. "I sought to harm him through the pretty little schemer Madame Bonacieux, for it would seem he has lost his heart to her. But she has been removed from the prison at Nantes where Rochefort placed her."

"By the queen's orders, no less," interposed the cardinal. "She is now at the convent of Béthune, where the queen had her secretly conveyed . . ."

There was a pause, a mumble of words, then milady's voice rang out: "Then you promise — I have your word, your eminence, that you will send D'Artagnan to the Bastille?"

"Only if you bring me proof of his connection with Buckingham."

"I will find you proof ten times over!" replied the countess, confidently.

Athos looked at his two friends. "We have heard enough," he said. "We must warn D'Artagnan . . ."

When the three musketeers returned to camp, they sought out D'Artagnan and drew him aside.

"You must take great care," Athos began, "or you will shortly find yourself in the Bastille, my friend . . ."

Then he explained all that had taken place in the upper room of the inn.

"Nothing matters!" cried D'Artagnan, when he had heard him out, "compared with the news you bring me of my sweet Madame Bonacieux. She lives! She is at Béthune! Where do you suppose that is?"

"Why, upon the frontiers of Artois and Flanders," his friend told him. "When the siege is over, we shall go there."

The end of the affair

THE SIEGE OF Rochelle dragged on while D'Artagnan fumed with impatience to be on his way to the convent.

His impatience was increased by his fears for Madame Bonacieux's safety, should the Comtesse de Winter reach Béthune before he did. His beloved would have no reason to suspect the countess's evil designs upon her.

Finally, it was M. de Tréville, captain of the musketeers, who eventually secured the release from duty of the four friends. Soon, mounted on fast horses, they found themselves at last on the road to Béthune.

Meanwhile, milady had delivered Richelieu's message to the duke in England, and was now back in France,

determined to reach Madame Bonacieux before D'Artagnan.

The gracious reception accorded her by the abbess on her arrival at the convent assured her that D'Artagnan had not been there. And in a few moments, she was seated in the parlour awaiting Madame Bonacieux. She entered the room wearing the habit of a novice, and the countess, pretending the warmest friendship, rose, took her hand, and said, "I come from M. D'Artagnan. The cardinal knows you are here. You must come away with me. It is what D'Artagnan wishes. We will hide until he comes for you."

Madame Bonacieux stared at her visitor, longing to believe that D'Artagnan had indeed sent such a message, yet

apprehensive lest the strange woman could be tricking her.

"Believe me, I *am* your friend," continued the countess. "Come, pull yourself together. Drink some wine to give you strength for our journey, and let us go."

Intense panic overcame the young woman, and she sank into a chair. The countess poured out a small glass of Spanish wine for her. But just as she was putting the glass to her lips, the sound of horsemen approaching reached her ears.

The countess ran to the window. It was light enough for her to recognize those who were coming. She saw the glitter of laced hats and the waving of plumes, and uttered a stifled groan as she saw D'Artagnan.

"Come on, do come on!" she urged, running to Madame Bonacieux and striving to drag her to the door. "It's the cardinal's guards!"

"I cannot," Madame Bonacieux gasped. "My strength fails me."

A strange light came into the countess's eyes as the young woman collapsed again into the chair. She ran to the table, poured into the glass some powder concealed in a ring she was wearing, then handed the glass to the frightened Madame Bonacieux, who drank mechanically.

Satisfied, and with a look of gloating triumph she rushed from the room, while

almost at the same moment D'Artagnan and the three musketeers entered by another door.

D'Artagnan fell upon his knees before the pale young woman, who was slumped lifelessly in the chair.

"Have I found you — only to lose you in death?" he murmured anxiously.

At the sound of his voice, she opened her eyes. Before she could speak, Athos cried, "Madame, tell me in heaven's name, is this empty glass yours?"

"Mine, sir," said the young woman, feebly. "She poured out the wine for me. Such a beautiful lady, the Comtesse de Winter . . . She came . . ." Suddenly, they saw the color drain from her face. Her body stiffened, and all watching knew that she had died.

D'Artagnan buried his head in his hands, sobbing bitterly, while his three friends turned away in sympathy.

Meanwhile, having wrought the most painful vengeance possible on

D'Artagnan, the evil countess made her way to Armentières, where she had a rendezvous with Rochefort.

Satisfied that she was safe from pursuit, she rented a lonely cottage on the outskirts of the town, and prepared to wait for the cardinal's agent.

It was there some days later, that D'Artagnan and the three musketeers took her captive.

There was no denying that she had brought about the death of Madame Bonacieux by poison or that she had led a life of despicable crime. At her trial she was sentenced to execution, a punishment she richly deserved.

For a long time after these events, D'Artagnan remained sunk in deep melancholy. But when, at last, his commission as a lieutenant in the musketeers was approved, his spirits revived, and he

became the swashbuckling D'Artagnan of old again. He fought three times with his old enemy, Rochefort, and wounded him three times. Then, with honor satisfied, he declared he would fight him no more.

And what of the three musketeers who had so ably supported him in all his adventures?

After the surrender of Rochelle, Aramis finally turned his back on soldiering and entered a monastery. Porthos married a rich widow and settled down to lead a far quieter existence, and Athos, after some time, quit the service to manage a small estate which he had inherited.

So D'Artagnan alone remained in the king's service — a true musketeer to the end.